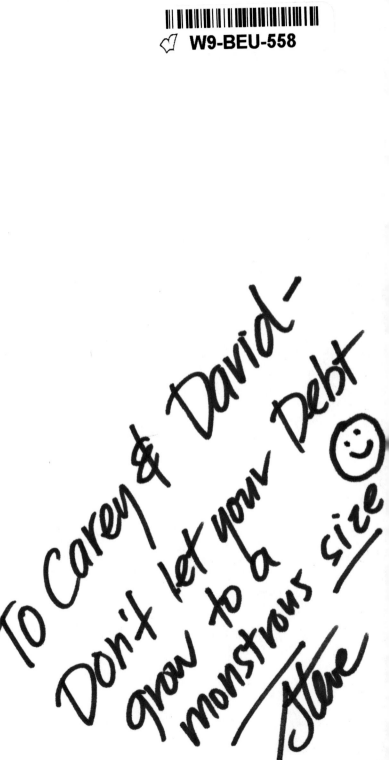

To Carey & David -

Don't let your Debt

grow to a

monstrous size ☺

Steve

THE DANGEROUS PET

by Thomas F. Siems

Illustrated by Steven G. Blye

Book One
A Series of Dangerous Decisions

To order additional books, please contact:
Xlibris Corporation
A Strategic Partner of Random House Ventures
Philadelphia, PA
1-888-795-4274
www.Xlibris.com
Orders@Xlibris.com

DEDICATION

To Margi Siems and Barbara Blye,
Our beautiful brides!

And to our awesome children,
In the Siems family: Christin, Megan, Alec and TJ,
And in the Blye family: Eric, DJ, Ty, Alex and Marie.

We couldn't have completed these words and drawings
without your inspiration, patience and loving support!

I peered in the window. I liked it a lot.
I just had to have it—that big blue robot!

But how would I get it? And what would it take?
I looked at the price tag and got a headache!

I knew that I needed a big wad of money.
But where would I get it? No, this was not funny!

I took time to think and develop a plan.
Would Dad give me cash? Would he be a good man?

That big blue robot. What a thing! What a toy!
I knew it would bring me great fun and such joy!

My dreams were of rides and of games we could play.
But deep in my mind I saw no way to pay!

Next morning I saw him—a man with a box.
I saw him sit down in the park on some rocks.

He opened the box as he turned a small knob,
And out hopped a meek little, green furry blob!

The blob, it was starved—like a bear seeking honey.
I gasped when I saw that the man fed it *money!*

He held out three coins and then threw them up high.
The blob leapt to eat them then gave a big sigh.

He walked to his car, and it followed him back.
But would it be nice or turn 'round and attack?

His trunk was stuffed full, with a blob in each cage.
But feeding them money must take a big wage!

Just then I remembered the toy in the store.
I wanted to have it, yet not do a chore.

No cleaning, no mopping, no robbing a bank;
I yearned for that robot so much my heart sank.

I had to get money, and needed it fast.
But where would I get some? That toy might not last!

I shouted, "That robot would be so darn cool!"
The man heard me yelling and started to drool.

He held up some papers and said with such grace,
"If you need some money, I know just the place."

He added that if I would care for his blob,
That I could get money, yet not have a job!

Is this really true? Could there be such a deal?
I got so excited I did a cartwheel!

He said that he had lots of
money for me.
But didn't I learn once that
nothing is free?

And how can I get all
the money I need,
Yet not have to work
or perform a good deed?

He promised me money
on just one condition:
I must take his box and
complete a big mission.

"Now care for this wonderful, green furry pet. It lives in this box and goes by the name *Debt*."

"It eats only money—three coins every day. That keeps it quite happy and out of your way."

"Just three coins are needed,
not one and not two.
You must feed it daily,
whatever you do!"

"The contract is clear
on how Debt should be fed.
Just don't miss a meal or
it grows and turns red!"

"Now this may sound scary,
but one thing is true:
Just sign here, then take
home the robot that's blue!"

I thought for a moment
of what could go wrong . . .
I wanted that robot!
My greed was so strong!

We signed all the papers and shook on the deal,
Then he gave me cash and the box made of steel.

I could not believe it! The toy was now mine!
And WOW! that was simple—*just sign on the line!*

I started back home with my robot and Debt.
It could not get better—a toy AND a pet!

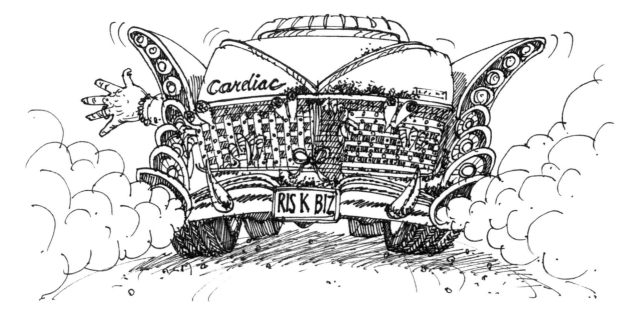

My robot could talk; he could dance and could think. He did many tricks with a smile and a wink.

But Debt made me worry as time went along.
The coins in my bank would too soon all be gone!

My Debt was still eating three coins every day.
But I thought there must be a much cheaper way.

I spoke to my robot and asked what to do.
He said, "Why not try to just feed the Debt TWO?"

I gave Debt two coins and then watched as it ate.
And to my surprise saw its eyes fill with hate!

My Debt became creepy and nasty and mean!
With claws and big fangs and huge eyes that were green!

It screeched and it yelled and it made lots of chatter.
And when it rolled over, it seemed so much fatter!

I got very scared and hid under my bed.
Oh, what would I do if it turned a bright red?

I picked up my bank and just knew I should pray,
For no coins were found to my frightened dismay.

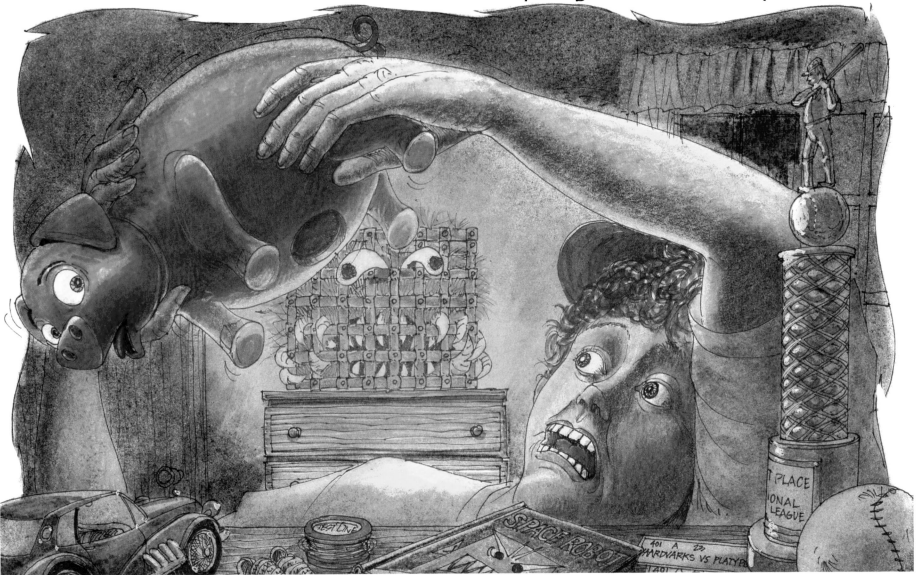

Yes, I was in trouble. Now what should I do?
I could not feed Debt. Could this really be true?

And when I told Debt I ran out of its food,
It suddenly was in a very bad mood!

Debt got very angry and broke through the box!
Before I could act, it was big as an ox!

It turned a bright red and then grew to the sky.
I wished Debt were gone and I started to cry!

My Debt was so large! And I hadn't a clue.
I didn't know what in the world I could do!

My Debt was no longer a small, little thing.
It now took control as my Master and King!

And I could not sleep, and I felt very sick.
This Debt was enormous, and thick as a brick.

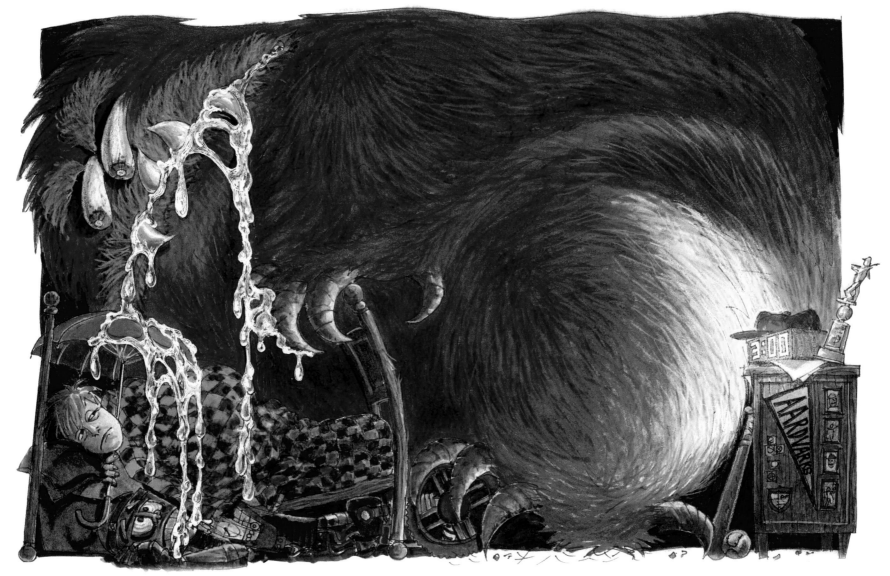

And 'cause of this Debt I no longer had fun.
I worried and fretted and wanted to run.

At last I could see that I needed some aid
As Debt broke the door and went on a tirade.

I called on the experts: my Dad and my Mom.
To give me some guidance and words of wisdom.

They asked if I knew all the dangers of Debt,
And if I could write down a simple budget.

They taught me that Debt is a duty to pay.
And only with feeding will it go away.

"Big Debt is a danger that makes you its slave.
You must feed it often to make it behave!"

"It's all right to borrow if you can repay . . .
And keep your Debt small, so it's out of your way."

"But be on your guard if you borrow to live.
For Debt will take over with nothing to give!"

"First make a sound budget, to know what you earn
And whether or not you have money to burn!"

"Save some of your cash for the times that are tough.
You might need it then, when you won't earn enough."

"Be careful with money. Don't make it your Master.
To want it too much leads to certain disaster."

"To get your Debt smaller, you must feed it more;
With plenty of money so it will not roar."

"Now where will you get all the money you need?
You must get a job! And get rid of your greed!"

"Now start in the backyard by mowing the grass . . . And washing the car and then shining the brass."

I earned a few dollars, enough to feed Debt;
And lessons I learned I will never forget.

I scrubbed and I cleaned and I straightened my room.
And when I fed Debt, I no longer felt doom.

Fed FIVE coins a day, and for week after week,
Debt shrank and got smaller 'til it could not speak!

And a funny thing happened one day as Debt ate—
It just disappeared without cleaning its plate!

So now when I see a neat toy in a store,
I'll plan and save money . . . unlike times before.

I'll make a sound budget because that is wise,
And won't let Debt grow to a monstrous size!

Thomas F. Siems. Ph.D. enjoys life, liberty and the pursuit of happiness! Tom is married to the beautiful, talented and fabulous Margi Facchini Siems. Both are native Michiganders turned Texan and have brought four children into the world: Christin (a playwright), Megan (a management scientist), Alec (an aspiring businessman) and TJ (a young genius).

Tom and Margi enjoy vacationing with family on the beach or in the mountains, watching action-thrillers, and staying active with their two energetic, loveable black lab puppies in Carrollton, Texas.

Tom spends most of his time as an economist at the Federal Reserve Bank of Dallas and as a lecturer in the Lyle School of Engineering at Southern Methodist University. He enjoys teaching audiences new insights, inspiring young people to greatness and being an optimistic dreamer (be on the lookout for The Dangerous Pet: The Musical).

Dr. Siems earned a BSE from The University of Michigan and MS and PhD degrees from SMU. He's the author of more than 50 academic and Federal Reserve publications, having his work covered in *The Wall Street Journal*, the *Financial Times* and *The Economist*. *The Dangerous Pet* is his fifth children's book.

Steven G. Blye has been drawing for fun since he can remember getting art supplies from his parents. His love of art encouraged him to sketch on everything that stood still, including his school assignments. Steve later provided illustrations for school yearbooks from junior high through college.

The scary words "starving artist" led him to study in the field of architecture at the University of Illinois and at a university near Paris, France. Starting his architectural career in Texas, where he also participated as an actor and set designer, he returned to Chicago and has spent the past twenty-five plus years designing hotels, hospitals, and other large edifices around the USA and internationally.

Secretly wishing he was in a studio painting or doing anything that did not require continual mental gymnastics, Steve burned some midnight oil to illustrate Tom's inspiring story, which have become his first drawings for a children's book. Steve lives in the suburbs of Chicago with his wife, Barbara, and their five children, Eric, DJ, Ty, Alex, and Marie.